Night Shift

Jessie Hartland

BLOOMSBURY
CHILDREN'S
BOOKS

BUS STOP

Late at night when
the owls are out
and the raccoons are
diving into trash cans,

and you are finishing up the
last bit of chocolate pudding
and then brushing your teeth
and wishing you didn't have
to go to bed just yet,

there are people out there
awake doing all sorts
of interesting things . . .

They are on the
NIGHT SHIFT.

What is that swishing
sound outside?

THE STREET SWEEPER!

At 10:00 in the evening,
when the streets empty out,
the street sweeper
swishes along
down the roads.

Leaning way out,
the driver skillfully
edges up against the curb.

Brushes spinning,
they twist and turn,
swivel and swirl
to get every bit:

candy wrappers, a lost mitten,
acorns, leaves, paper cups,
and other trash all get
sucked up by the big sweeper.

Who does the street sweeper
stop to watch so late at night?

WINDOW DRESSERS!

The fancy store is closed, and the doors are locked; the last shoppers are long gone. It's 11:00.

Here come the window dressers! With their team of trusty mannequins and their feathers, felt, and fluff, they will revamp the windows and make shoppers grin and giggle.

GREEN is the new BLACK

A kitty made of pickles,
a topiary poodle,
a mannequin dressed
smartly with a wig
of spinach noodles!

Who keeps the window dressers whistling in the wee hours?

THE LATE-NIGHT RADIO DJ!

Disc jockeys are the voices that talk to us through the radio.

They choose the songs and play them.

They also report the news: "A UFO has landed at the gas station!"

And make very important announcements:

"Do you like CHEESE? There is a Gouda-eating contest coming up on Thursday . . ."

They tell us the time and weather: "It's 11:30 p.m. and 53 degrees . . . Is anyone out there listening?"

Who likes to request his favorite songs late at night?

THE SECURITY GUARD!

At the closed and quiet
Modern Art Museum
the security guard is
making the rounds.

No visitors here at 11:45;
this job is about protecting
the priceless artwork.

Wait! There's a rustling
sound! Turn down the radio.

Check all doors and windows!
Monitor all surveillance
systems! Test alarms,
sensors, and infrared
detector function!

No paintings are askew;
no sculptures are wobbling.
Look—it's just a mouse!

Who calls the guard just
before midnight to chat?

THE NEWSPAPER PRINTER!

Reporters write about
the news all day;
printers print
their stories all night.

The huge printing press
needs tweaking.
Stop the presses!
There's a JAM!

Reload the paper,
ink the presses.
Feed the paper,
adjust ink flow.

Trim, assemble,
fold, and bundle.
It's 12:05 a.m.

Darkness still lingers
as the daily paper
is delivered
to your front door.

Whose late-night work
outside the window
distracts the printer?

BRIDGE PAINTERS!

On a cool, dry night
bridge painters assemble
to climb the massive
suspension bridge.

Step-by-step they clip
and reclip their safety belts.
Nets are below to catch
those who might fall.

At the tower's top
is an enormous nest:
a hawk with three eggs
are painted around.

Some paint drips down
but the traffic is light.
Not many cars out
so late at night.

Whose car gets
splattered passing over
a dripping bridge
at 1:00 a.m.?

THE ZOOKEEPER!

On her way to the zoo,
where the animals are
sleeping in darkness.

But one hall is bright.
Who sleeps in bright light?
Nocturnal animals, that's who.

Every night at the zoo, in
a bright space all their own,
these animals are tricked
into thinking it's day,
when they like to sleep!

A bulb's just burned out and
an owl-monkey's stirring . . .
Quick! Change that bulb
and send her back sleeping.

So one day when you visit
the "World of Night" hall,
you'll see active nocturnal
animals, not sleepy at all!

Who's driving a
shipment of ocelots
bound for the zoo?

THE FREIGHTER CAPTAIN!

The freighter boat plods along,
cruising the great ocean
from South America,
carrying huge containers filled
with perishable freight of all kinds:
bananas, cocoa pods,
mangoes, sardines,
coconuts, and ocelots.

Boat captain at the
wheel, gazing ahead.
Radar, navigational
charts, GPS*, and a
compass keep her on
course.

*global positioning system

The steward brings up
a tuna sandwich and a
cup of coffee at 2:00 a.m.
That and some salty wind
refresh the captain.

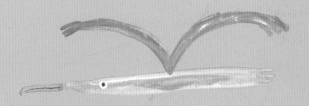

Seagulls up ahead!
Land must be near!

Who takes the ocelots
from the ocean pier
to the inland zoo?

THE TRUCK DRIVER!

Under an inky-black sky
the truck driver
swiftly loads up
perishable freight
just arrived
from South America:

coconuts going to Kansas,
mangoes to Iowa,
cocoa pods to California.

Don't load the sardines
next to the ocelots!

THE ROAD WORKER!

At 3:00 in the morning
road workers meet to mend
a broken highway.

Bumps, humps,
lumps, potholes,
bulges, and cracks
need to be fixed.

A backhoe breaks
up the old road.
A grader spreads
out the new one.
A roller rolls it smooth.

Traffic is light but still
a bottleneck has formed:
three lanes into one.

What a mess!
But better to fix it now
than at rush hour.

Who does the road
worker visit for
a snack at 3:30 a.m.?

THE DONUT BAKER!

Delicious donuts
there for you in the morn.
How so fresh?
They make them at night.

Flour and milk mixed,
sugar and yeast added;
dough is stirred,
donut shapes formed,
dropped into hot oil.
They deep-fry and
drain on the side.

Cream-filled? Sprinkley?
Tutti-frutti co-co?
Caramel-mint or
pistachio rococo?
Broccoli-nut, healthy
whole wheat?

Which one will she sample
on her 4:00 a.m. break?

Who bought a BIG
box of donuts
for a nighttime voyage?

THE FISHERMAN!

Fishermen out
on a cool, dark night,
on the lookout for fish.
"There's a school!"

Spread the net.
Corral the fish.
Gather the net.
The winch hauls it up.

A big catch!
Plenty of fresh fish to sell
at the morning fish market.

Coasting through the
darkness,
on the way to port.

The last donut has been eaten.

There's a lighthouse up ahead, and the fog is rolling in!

Who comes to the rescue when the fishermen run aground at 5:00 a.m.?

THE TUGBOAT CAPTAIN!

Sturdy tugboat,
low to the water,
helps big boats
come into and out of port.

The captain eases her up to
the grounded fishing boat
coming in at sunrise
at a low, low tide.

All engine, the tugboat gently nudges the fishing boat along, off the sandbar.

Unlike the big, unwieldy trawler, the tugboat is easily maneuverable, sure and strong in any direction.

"Last job of the night."
"Let's go for coffee."
It's morning!

Who serves coffee to the tugboat captain and all of his friends?

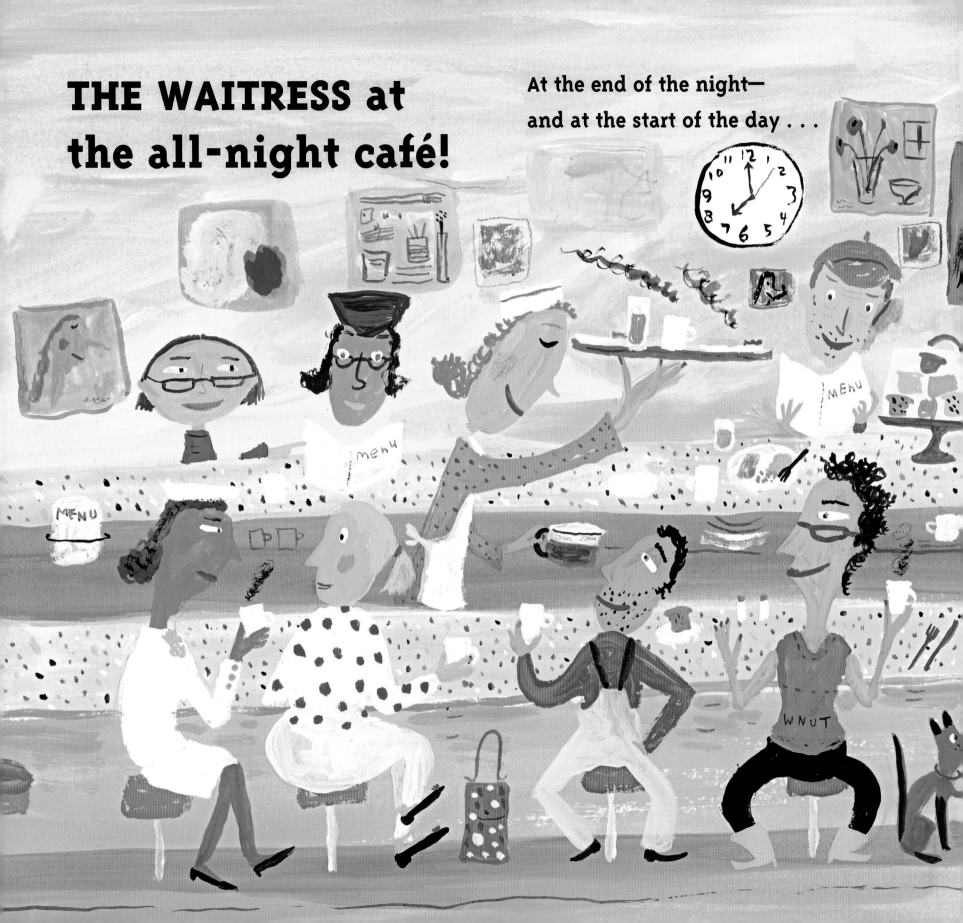

THE WAITRESS at the all-night café!

At the end of the night—
and at the start of the day . . . .

... the
NIGHT SHIFT
meets at the
all-night café!

For my lovely niece, Annabel, a nonstop writer of poems, prose, and comics, day and night.

Thanks to Laura Walker and Margaret Juntwait
for letting me take a peek at WNYC radio.

Typeset in Triplex Serif
Art created with gouache
Book design by Nicole Gastonguay

Published by Bloomsbury U.S.A. Children's Books
175 Fifth Avenue, New York, NY 10010
Distributed to the trade by Holtzbrinck Publishers

Library of Congress Cataloging-in-Publication Data
Hartland, Jessie.
Night shift / by Jessie Hartland. — 1st U.S. ed.
        p.   cm.
Summary: Late at night after children have gone to bed, people who work the night shift,
like street sweepers, window dressers, newspaper printers, road workers, and donut bakers,
are doing their jobs.
ISBN-13: 978-1-59990-025-4 • ISBN-10: 1-59990-025-4 (hardcover)
ISBN-13: 978-1-59990-138-1 • ISBN-10: 1-59990-138-2 (reinforced)
[1. Occupations—Fiction. 2. Night—Fiction.] I. Title.
PZ7.H2638Ni 2007   [E]—dc22   2006102092

First U.S. Edition 2007
Printed in Malaysia
1 3 5 7 9 10 8 6 4 2 (hardcover)
1 3 5 7 9 10 8 6 4 2 (reinforced)

All papers used by Bloomsbury U.S.A. are natural, recyclable products
made from wood grown in well-managed forests. The manufacturing processes
conform to the environmental regulations of the country of origin.

gladys

TO: ZOO
LIVE animals
From: South America

E
Hartland, Jessie.
Night shift /

Printer's
INK

375°

siberian SQUIRREL #6